Senses
on the
Farm

Shelley Rotner

Millbrook Press   Minneapolis

To the farmers, our local heroes,
with special thanks to Chip Parsons
and the Parsons Farm

Millbrook Press
A division of Lerner Publishing Group, Inc.
241 First Avenue North
Minneapolis, MN 55401 U.S.A.

Website address: www.lernerbooks.com

Library of Congress Cataloging-in-Publication Data

Rotner, Shelley.
    Senses on the farm / by Shelley Rotner.
        p.   cm.
    ISBN 978-0-8225-8623-4 (lib. bdg. : alk. paper)
    1. Senses and sensation—Juvenile literature. 2. Farms—Juvenile
literature. I. Title.
QP434.R663 2009
612.8—dc22   2007044371

Manufactured in the United States of America
1 2 3 4 5 6 – DP – 14 13 12 11 10 09

On the farm...

Hear a tractor
plowing the field.

Touch the warm soil, ready for planting seeds.

See the corn growing

higher

and higher.

Smell
spring flowers in bloom.

Hear the bee buzzing.

See a newborn goat trying to walk.

Touch
the hairy coat
of a piglet.

See the
calf's big ears.

Touch the soft, woolly fur of a lamb.

Smell the newly cut hay.

Hear a hungry horse chomp.

Hear the cows mooing

and
chewing.

Touch the cow's rough tongue.

Taste the farm-fresh milk.

Smell the pigpen

and the farm animals' manure.

Taste
a hand-picked
strawberry.

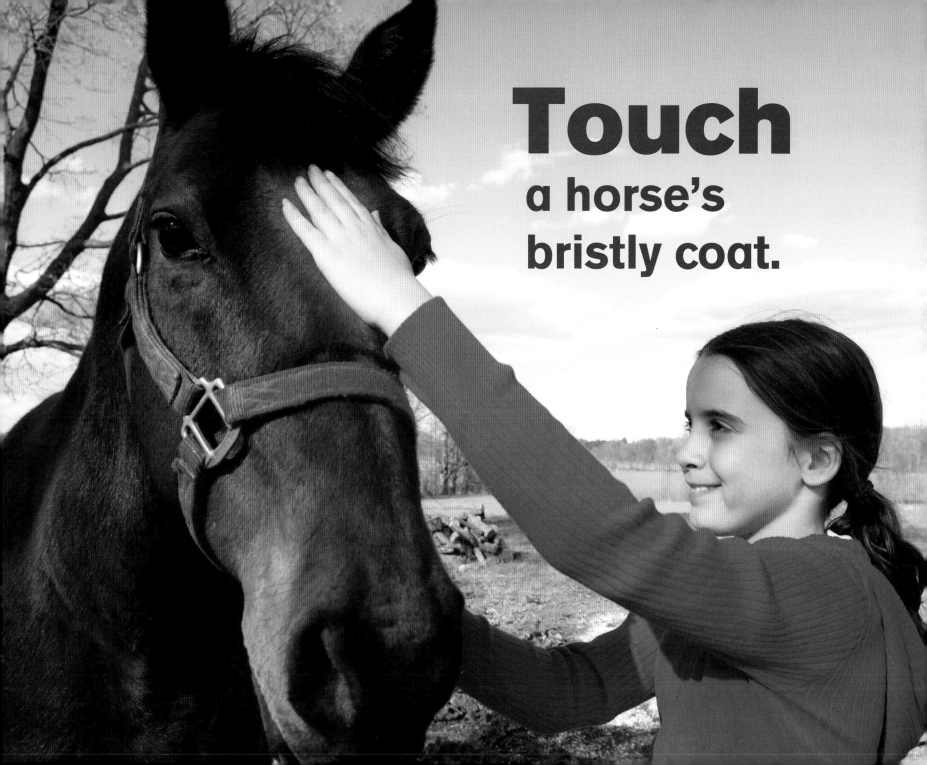

Touch
a horse's
bristly coat.

Hear the hens cluck.

Touch
a smooth,
oval egg.

See the farmer harvesting corn.

Taste
the fresh corn
on the cob.

See the fall pumpkins growing on their vines.

Taste
a crisp, juicy
apple from an
apple tree.

See the stand where the farmer sells fresh fruits and vegetables.

SWEET
DUMPLING

69¢ lb

SWEET TENDER FLESH JUST
SLICE IN HALF AND BAKE
WITH OUR MAPLE SYRUP

DELICATA

69¢ lb

BEST WHEN STUFFED
OR BAKED WITH OUR
MAPLE SYRUP

Carnival

69¢ lb.

See the tall, round silos where the corn is stored for the winter.

On the farm, there's so much to see, hear, smell, taste, touch.